The Tale of Despereaux™

The Mouse and the Princess

Based on the motion picture screenplay by Gary Ross
Based on the book by Kate DiCamillo

CANDLEWICK PRESS

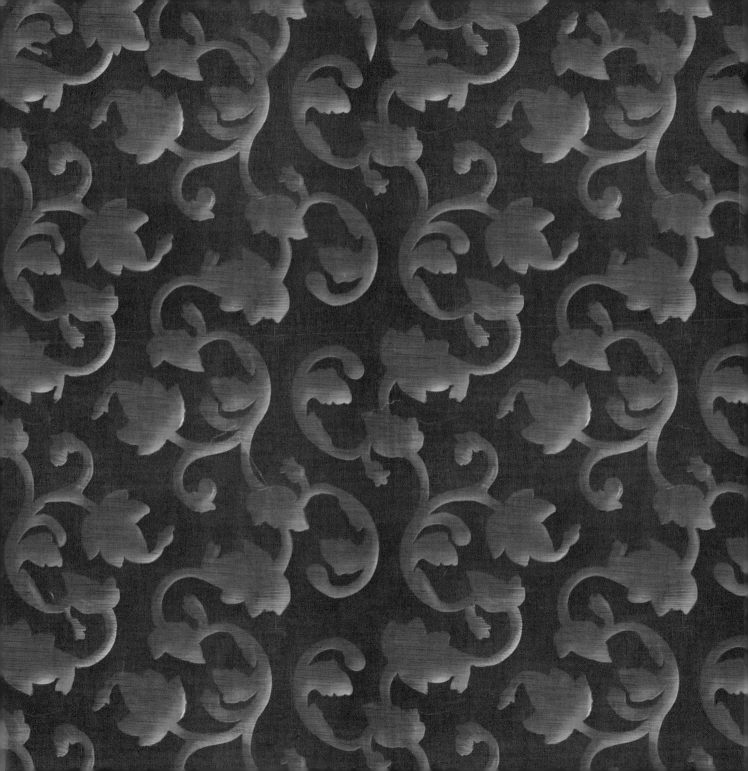

From the moment he was born, Despereaux Tilling was a mouse like no other. His eyes were wide open, and he looked right up at the light, which seemed to shine down on him alone. His exceptionally large ears moved and flexed. They looked almost *curious*.

The newborn mouse looked all around him. He noticed everything in the room. On the walls he saw something most extraordinary — words. Rows and rows, and pages and pages of words. He couldn't stop looking at them.

His mother, father, and brother gathered at the bassinet with the doctor to admire the new baby.

"Mom, he's so puny!" said his brother, Furlough. "And look at those ears!"

It was true Despereaux was different. Despite his tiny size, he heard more, saw more, and experienced more than any of the other mice.

As Despereaux grew older — but not much bigger — he came to love books. He was reading about a princess one day when he heard strange, sad music. It was the mournful strumming of the king's guitar. Despereaux followed the sound. Inside a nearby chamber he came upon a princess. Her name was Princess Pea, and she was lovely, more beautiful than even the storybook princess.

But there were tears in her eyes.

"Why are you crying?" Despereaux asked.

"Oh!" she said, frightened for just a moment. "Are you a rat?"

"No," replied Despereaux.

She asked, "What are you, a mouse?"

Despereaux doffed his hat. "I am a gentleman," he said.

Pea smiled and leaned a little closer. "Well, how do you do?"

Despereaux could see that Princess Pea longed for something. He knew that this was the cause of her sadness. He told her about the storybook princess, how she, too, lived in a castle, and how she, too, had a great sadness.

"How does this story end?" asked the princess.

Despereaux had not yet finished the story. He didn't know what happened to the fairy-tale princess.

"Will you promise to read the rest of the story and tell me how it ends?" asked Princess Pea.

Despereaux promised.

"You are a very brave mouse," she said. She kissed her finger and touched it lightly to Despereaux's nose. "Thank you, my good gentleman."

Back in his room, Despereaux couldn't wait to tell his brother all about the princess.

"She was beautiful," he said. "Like an angel."

"You are crazy!" said Furlough. "You can't talk to a human! It's the worst thing you can do."

"No," answered Despereaux. "It's the best thing I ever did."

"They'll throw you in the dungeon," cried Furlough. "You'll get eaten by rats!"

"It would be worth it," said Despereaux.

When the Mouse Council learned what he had done, Despereaux *was* thrown in the dungeon, where he barely escaped being eaten by rats.

Despereaux could hear things that others could not. It was only he who heard a cry for help from somewhere deep within the dungeon. He knew that soft, lovely voice—it was Princess Pea! She had been kidnapped and was being hidden in a prison cell. Despereaux raced to her side.

"I will deliver you from this evil, ma'am," he vowed.

Despereaux thought about the royal library. He remembered the story about a brave knight who sets out to rescue a beautiful princess.

Despereaux knew what he had to do.

He hurried back upstairs and into the kitchen. There he found a needle for a sword and Boldo, a genie made of pots and pans. Together they returned to the dungeon and battled the rats. Finally, the rats slunk into the shadows and Princess Pea was saved.

Despereaux was not like other mice.
He was truly a brave knight.
He had courage, chivalry, honor,
and the love of a princess.

First edition 2008

Library of Congress Cataloging-in-Publication Data is available.
Library of Congress Catalog Card Number 2008927403
ISBN 978-0-7636-4077-4

2 4 6 8 10 9 7 5 3 1

Printed in Mexico

This book was typeset in Garamond Ludlow.
The illustrations were created digitally.

Candlewick Press
99 Dover Street
Somerville, Massachusetts 02144

visit us at www.candlewick.com